What Wally Wanted

Level 6A

Written by Louise Goodman
Illustrated by Kate Daubney

What is synthetic phonics?

Synthetic phonics teaches children to recognise the sounds of letters and to blend (synthesise) them together to make whole words.

Understanding sound/letter relationships gives children the confidence and ability to read unfamiliar words, without having to rely on memory or guesswork; this helps them to progress towards independent reading.

Did you know? Spoken English uses more than 40 speech sounds. Each sound is called a *phoneme*. Some phonemes relate to a single letter (d-o-g) and others to combinations of letters (sh-ar-p). When a phoneme is written down it is called a *grapheme*. Teaching these sounds, matching them to their written form and sounding out words for reading is the basis of synthetic phonics.

Consultant

I love reading phonics has been created in consultation with language expert Abigail Steel. She has a background in teaching and teacher training and is a respected expert in the field of synthetic phonics. Abigail Steel is a regular contributor to educational publications. Her international education consultancy supports parents and teachers in the promotion of literacy skills.

Reading tips

This book focuses on two sounds made with the letter a: a as in hat and o as in what.

Tricky words in this book

Any words in bold may have unusual spellings or are new and have not yet been introduced.

> ### Tricky word in this book:
>
> ## **walked**

Extra ways to have fun with this book

After the reader has read the story, ask them questions about what they have just read:

What was the first thing Wally swapped?
Can you find two words which contain the different sounds shown by the letter a?

Who is your favourite character in the book?

A pronunciation guide

This grid contains the sounds used in the stories in levels 4, 5 and 6 and a guide on how to say them. /**a**/ represents the sounds made, rather than the letters in a word.

/**ai**/ as in game	/**ai**/ as in play/they	/**ee**/ as in leaf/these	/**ee**/ as in he
/**igh**/ as in kite/light	/**igh**/ as in find/sky	/**oa**/ as in home	/**oa**/ as in snow
/**oa**/ as in cold	/**y+oo**/ as in cube/music/new	long /**oo**/ as in flute/crew/blue	/**oi**/ as in boy
/**er**/ as in bird/hurt	/**or**/ as in snore/oar/door	/**or**/ as in dawn/sauce/walk	/**e**/ as in head
/**e**/ as in said/any	/**ou**/ as in cow	/**u**/ as in touch	/**air**/ as in hare/bear/there
/**eer**/ as in deer/here/cashier	/**t**/ as in tripped/skipped	/**d**/ as in rained	/**j**/ as in gent/gin/gym
/**j**/ as in barge/hedge	/**s**/ as in cent/circus/cyst	/**s**/ as in prince	/**s**/ as in house
/**ch**/ as in itch/catch	/**w**/ as in white	/**h**/ as in who	/**r**/ as in write/rhino

Sounds in this story are
highlighted in the grid.

/**f**/ as in phone	/**f**/ as in rough	/**ul**/ as in pencil/ hospital	/**z**/ as in fries/ cheese/breeze
/**n**/ as in knot/ gnome/engine	/**m**/ as in welcome /thumb/column	/**g**/ as in guitar/ghost	/**zh**/ as in vision/beige
/**k**/ as in chord	/**k**/ as in plaque/ bouquet	/**nk**/ as in uncle	/**ks**/ as in box/books/ ducks/cakes
/**a**/ and /**o**/ as in hat/what	/**e**/ and /**ee**/ as in bed/he	/**i**/ and /**igh**/ as in fin/find	/**o**/ and /**oa**/ as in hot/cold
/**u**/ and short /**oo**/ as in but/put	/**ee**/, /**e**/ and /**ai**/ as in eat/ bread/break	/**igh**/, /**ee**/ and /**e**/ as in tie/field/friend	/**ou**/ and /**oa**/ as in cow/blow
/**ou**/, /**oa**/ and /**oo**/ as in out/ shoulder/could	/**i**/ and /**ai**/ as in money/they	/**c**/ and /**s**/ as in cat/cent	/**y**/, /**igh**/ and /**i**/ as in yes/sky/myth
/**g**/ and /**j**/ as in got/giant	/**ch**/, /**c**/ and / **sh**/ as in chin/ school/chef	/**er**/, /**air**/ and /**eer**/ as in earth/bear/ears	/**u**/, /**ou**/ and /**oa**/ as in plough/dough

Be careful not to add an 'uh' sound to 's', 't', 'p',
'c', 'h', 'r', 'm', 'd', 'g', 'l', 'f' and 'b'. For example,
say 'fff' not 'fuh' and 'sss' not 'suh'.

Wally and his black cat were
wandering along.

Wally wanted some gold. But all he had was a ball.

Wally **walked** along and saw
an acrobat.
"Do you have any gold?"
Wally asked.

"All I have is this sack. I'll swap
it for your ball."
Wally swapped the ball for
the sack.

Wally walked along and saw an
animal tamer.
"Do you have any gold?"
Wally asked.

"All I have is this bat. I'll swap it
for your sack."
Wally swapped the sack for
the bat.

Wally walked along and saw
an alligator.
"Do you have any gold?" Wally
asked.

"All I have is this watch. I'll swap it for your bat."
Wally swapped the bat for the watch.

Wally walked along and saw
an actor.
"Do you have any gold?"
Wally asked.

"All I have is this pie. I'll swap it
for your watch."
Wally swapped the watch for
the pie.

Wally walked along and saw
a witch.
"Do you have any gold?"
Wally asked.

"No. But I'll swap you one
spell for your black cat."

Wally looked at the black cat.
The black cat looked at Wally.

What Wally wanted was his
black cat!

Wally did not have any gold...
but he did have his friend.

Wally was very glad.

Wally gave his black cat a pat.

Then they ate the pie together.

OVER 48 TITLES IN SIX LEVELS
Abigail Steel recommends...

Some titles from Level 4

I love reading phonics — **The Maze**
978-1-84898-559-9

I love reading phonics — **Fairy Fay's Bad Day**
978-1-84898-560-5

I love reading phonics — **Pirate School**
978-1-84898-566-7

Some titles from Level 5

I love reading phonics — **Snapped by Sam**
978-1-84898-561-2

I love reading phonics — **Max's Trip**
978-1-84898-562-9

I love reading phonics — **George the Genius Gerbil**
978-1-84898-567-4

Other titles to enjoy from Level 6

I love reading phonics — **Superhero Ed**
978-1-84898-564-3

I love reading phonics — **Adine's Igloo**
978-1-84898-569-8

I love reading phonics — **The Robot Bop**
978-1-84898-570-4

An Hachette UK Company
www.hachette.co.uk

Copyright © Octopus Publishing Group Ltd 2012
First published in Great Britain in 2012 by TickTock, an imprint of Octopus Publishing Group Ltd,
Endeavour House, 189 Shaftesbury Avenue, London WC2H 8JY.
www.octopusbooks.co.uk

ISBN 978 1 84898 563 6

Printed and bound in China
10 9 8 7 6 5 4 3 2 1